LITTLE BLUE HOUSE BESIDE THE SEA

Jo Ellen Bogart

Art by
Carme Lemniscates

TILBURY HOUSE PUBLISHERS, THOMASTON, MAINE

There is a special place for me,

a little blue house beside the sea.

It nestles on its cliff so high
and watches as the boats go by.

Long grass dances in the breeze.
Flowers feed the honey bees.

I walk the cliff path every day
and watch as nature has its way.

Puffins waddle on the hills
with drooping fishes in their bills,

and in the distance, in the bay,
I see humpback whales at play.

The moon comes up, shining bright,
glistening on the sea at night.

A soft wind blows from out at sea
and brings the smell of brine to me.

The lighthouse towers, tall and white,
to show the ships its warning light.

And when a gale begins to blow,
I watch the storm-tossed waves below,

then hurry from the raging tide
to shelter in the warmth inside . . .

. . . my tiny house so strong and tight
that keeps me from the storm winds' might.

There is no place so dear to me
as that little blue house beside the sea.

A Note from Jo Ellen

As a child, I lived near the Gulf of Mexico where it touches the shores of Texas. I loved walking in the surf and feeling the retreating waves suck sand from beneath my toes. I liked the salty smell of the air, and I liked seeing ships far out on the water. When ships disappeared over the horizon, I wondered where they were going and what was out there. Later, I learned that the gulf opens into the great Atlantic Ocean, which laps the shores of faraway countries. Were other children dipping their toes in Atlantic water at the same time as me? The thought connected me with the great, wide, wonderful world.

Now I live in interior Canada. Though I am no longer close to an ocean, I know that the oceans, the world's seas, are more important than I once understood. Covering three-quarters of our planet's surface, they are home to an amazing variety of plants and animals, including many we have yet to discover.

What happens in the oceans is critically important to life on Earth. The oceans are vast, almost too big to imagine, yet they are not big enough to be immune from harm. The oceans have been called the lungs of the earth because phytoplankton, the tiny plants that live there, make much of the oxygen that is needed by living things on land as well as in the sea. If we pollute the oceans, overload them with plastic waste, heat them, and make them more acidic, the animals and plants that live there will sicken and die. All life on Earth is interconnected. All plants and animals need each other to survive and be healthy.

The little blue house in this book is in Newfoundland, on the eastern coast of Canada, facing the wide North Atlantic. I have stood on those shores and gazed out over the waters, thinking about all the places a boat could carry me. Could it take me to other little blue houses on faraway shores? Are the people in those houses gazing back across the sea toward me? Could they be my friends, people who love the ocean as I do and want to keep it safe, alive, and beautiful? I hope so. I believe so.

Text © 2020 by Jo Ellen Bogart · Illustrations © 2020 by Carme Lemniscates · Hardcover ISBN 978-0-88448-671-8 · First hardcover printing May 2020 · Tilbury House Publishers Thomaston, Maine 04861 · www.tilburyhouse.com · All rights reserved. No part of this publication may be reproduced or transmitted in any form or by any means, electronic or mechanical, including photocopying, recording, or any information storage or retrieval system, without permission in writing from the publisher. Library of Congress Control Number: 2020933511 · Designed by Frame25 Productions · Printed in Korea · 15 16 17 18 19 20 XXX 10 9 8 7 6 5 4 3 2 1

Carme created this book's mixed-media illustrations with monotypes, watercolors, acrylics, collage, and computer work.

Jo Ellen Bogart has written 20 books for young readers, including *The White Cat and the Monk*, which was named a Best Poetry Book by the National Council of Teachers of English. Her bestselling books include *Jeremiah Learns to Read, Daniel's Dog,* and *Gifts.* Jo Ellen has won the Ruth Schwartz Award and has been shortlisted for the Mr. Christie's Book Award.

Carme Lemniscates is the author, illustrator and designer of several critically acclaimed children's books including *Trees* (2017), *Birds* (2019), *Seeds* (2020), and *El jardín mágico,* for which she won the 2017 SCBWI Crystal Kite Award. She has also illustrated Jennifer Adams's *I Am a Warrior Goddess* (2018), Kate Coombs's *BabyLit Little Poets* board book series, and Hillary and Chelsea Clinton's *Grandma's Gardens* (2020). You can visit Carme at lemniscates.com.